The Christmas Gift

EMILY ARNOLD McCULLY

Harper & Row, Publishers—New York

The Christmas Gift

Copyright © 1988 by Emily Arnold McCully
Printed in the U.S.A. All rights reserved.
Typography by Bettina Rossner
10 9 8 7 6 5 4 3 2 1
First Edition

Library of Congress Cataloging-in-Publication Data
McCully, Emily Arnold.
    The Christmas gift.

    Summary: When a little mouse's treasured Christmas
gift is broken, Grandpa consoles her with a toy train
from his own childhood.
    [1. Mice—Fiction. 2. Christmas—Fiction. 3. Gifts—
Fiction. 4. Grandfathers—Fiction. 5. Stories without
words] I. Title.
PZ7.M13913Ch 1988   [E]   87-45758
ISBN 0-06-024211-6
ISBN 0-06-024212-4 (lib. bdg.)